A Random House PICTUREBACK® Book

Random House New York

rhcbooks.com

ISBN 978-0-525-57785-0

MANUFACTURED IN CHINA

10 9 8 7 6 5 4 3 2 1

Halloween Adventures!

CONTENTS

TRUCK or TREAT!

Adapted by David Lewman
Based on the teleplay "Truck or Treat" by Morgan von Ancken
Illustrated by Jason Fruchter

It was Halloween night in Axle City, and the Monster Machines were wearing their costumes. Starla was dressed as a witch. Zeg was a king. Stripes wore a pirate costume, and Darington was an octopus.

"Nice costumes, guys!" said Blaze, who was dressed as a knight.

Darington noticed something nearby.
"That guy's got a costume just like mine," he said.
"Darington," said Blaze, "that's not someone in a costume.
That's your shadow!" Blaze and AJ explained that when your body
blocks a light source, it makes a shadow.
The Monster Machines set down their candy buckets and made
shadows in Blaze's bright light. When AJ held up his superhero cape,
his shadow looked just like a big, spooky bat!

Meanwhile, Crusher and Pickle were driving by.

"Halloween is the best," said Pickle. "Just look at all the candy Blaze and his friends have!"

"Oooh, I want their candy!" Crusher whispered greedily. "And I know just how to get it."

Crusher built a machine that started sucking up everyone's candy buckets. But before long, the machine began to bulge and smoke. *KABOOM!* It blew up, shooting the buckets of candy into the sky.

Blaze and his friends drove off after the candy. Using his Visor View, AJ spotted it next to a barn outside Axle City.

"We've got to get to that barn before Crusher does!" Blaze said.

ZOOM! They roared off toward the barn.

There was a thick fog that night, and Stripes, Zeg, Starla, and Darington got separated from Blaze. They drove right into some big mud puddles.

"Oh, no!" cried Stripes. "This mud is really, really sticky!"

"Blaze!" they called. "HELP! We're stuck in the mud!"

"How are we going to save them, with all this fog?" asked AJ. "We can't even see where they are!"

Blaze had an idea. "Let's use shadows to find our friends," he said. "The light from the moon is shining down. And anything that blocks light makes a shadow."

One by one, Blaze spotted the shadows. He used a tow hook to pull his friends from the mud. The trucks were happy to be saved!

"Now we've got to get our candy back," Blaze said. The trucks raced into the night.

Suddenly, the trucks came to a screeching stop. Crusher had blocked the road with rocks! Zeg tried to push them out of the way, but they wouldn't budge.

Then AJ spotted a fallen tree limb. "I think there's something behind that branch," he said. He pushed it aside—and saw a tunnel!

"Come on, everybody," said Blaze. "This way!"

The trucks tried to race through the tunnel, but it was full of tickling spiders. Blaze and his friends were laughing so hard, they couldn't drive.

"Look!" exclaimed AJ. "Those spiders are making a giant web. We'll be trapped!"

VROOM! Everyone sped up and jumped through the web before it was finished.

"Great job, everyone!" said Blaze. "This way to our candy!"

Meanwhile, Crusher and Pickle had reached the barn—and the buckets of candy. They could hear Blaze and the other trucks zooming up behind them. Crusher had an idea to stop them: a Robo Pumpkin Launcher!

Pickle, who was now dressed as a shoe, stared at the machine. "I wonder what *that* does."

Suddenly, the machine began to hurl metal Robo Pumpkins into the sky . . . right at Blaze and his friends!

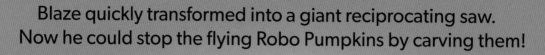

Blaze quickly transformed into a giant reciprocating saw.
Now he could stop the flying Robo Pumpkins by carving them!

Blaze and AJ cut up every Robo Pumpkin that flew their way!
"We came, we *sawed*, we conquered!" shouted Blaze.

Blaze and his friends finally reached the barn, but they had to get Crusher and Pickle away from the candy. Blaze decided to make a super-spooky shadow show. AJ raised his cape and stepped in front of Blaze's bright lights.

"Nothing can stop me from getting their candy now!" Crusher hooted. "Not Blaze, not his friends, not even . . . that giant spooky bat!"

Crusher and Pickle zoomed away as fast as their tires could carry them!

Blaze and his friends raced down to their buckets, where they all started gobbling up their candy with delight!

"Happy Halloween, Blaze!" said AJ as he grabbed his bucket.

"You too!" said Blaze, tossing candy into his mouth.

THE SPOOKY CABIN

Adapted by Tex Huntley

Based on the teleplay "Pups and the Ghost Cabin" by Scott Albert

Illustrated by Jason Fruchter

One day, Rocky and Rubble were helping their friend Jake repair a run-down cabin in the woods.

"This must have been a cool mining cabin," said Rocky.

"And once we fix it up, it will be a cool old *ski* cabin!" Jake replied.

It was time for lunch. But when Rubble opened his lunch box, he saw that his food was gone!

Jake said a ghost must have eaten it.

"Legend has it that the cabin is haunted by a hungry ghost," he explained.

Just then, Jake's lunch box rose from the porch and floated into the cabin!

Jake immediately called Ryder for help.

"Hey, Jake, we're here!" Ryder shouted when he and Chase rolled up to the cabin in their trucks.

Ryder turned on his flashlight and pushed open the cabin's creaky door.

"Hello? Is there a ghost in here?" he said.

Bats fluttered through the shadows as Ryder entered the dark cabin. Rocky and Rubble followed him nervously.

As they explored the gloomy cabin, Rubble found
a hidden door—and fell into a secret room!
The others didn't know where he'd gone.

"The ghost got him!" Rocky said.
But Ryder didn't believe in ghosts. He knew there had to be a logical explanation.

Outside, Chase's spy drone monitored the inside of the cabin.
He reported to Ryder that Rubble was still there.
"And he's not alone!" cried Chase.

It was getting really spooky in the cabin. Lights were flashing on and off. Doors rattled and pictures shook. And they heard Rubble howling for help!
"It sounds like Rubble is behind this wall," Ryder said.

Ryder found a switch and flipped it. The secret door opened, and Rubble tumbled out.

"Ryder, help!" Rubble shouted. "I mean . . . I wasn't scared."

Just then, Rocky saw some mice scurrying across the floor. "That explains the missing lunches," Ryder said.

The mice were the reason for the strange activities in the cabin.

"Look," Rocky said, "the mice are making the paintings move!"

"And they're making the lights flicker," Ryder added.

"And, hey—they're tickling my paws," Rubble said with a giggle.

To make sure the mice would stop "haunting" the cabin, Ryder and the pups built them a new house.

"They really like the peanut dispenser," Rubble said.

"Whenever you're in trouble, just *boo* for help!" Ryder exclaimed.

nickelodeon

SHIMMER AND SHINE

Monster Magic!

Adapted by Kristen L. Depken

Based on the teleplay "A Very Genie Halloweenie" by Whitney Fox

Illustrated by Dave Aikins

One night, Shimmer and Shine took their magic carpet to visit their friend Leah. When they appeared in her living room, they were inside a giant cauldron of candy.

"It's Halloween! You guys are going trick-or-treating with me!" Leah announced.

The friends visited Zac's house. He was dressed as a spider attached to a giant web.

"I got a little crazy with the glue, and now I'm stuck," he explained.

The girls pulled him down, and Leah introduced him to Shimmer and Shine.

"Those are some great genie costumes!" said Zac.

47

Zac was excited to show Leah and the genies the haunted-house decorations he'd made on his front lawn. There were tombstones made of pizza boxes and spooky-looking pumpkins. He had even put a mask on his dog, Rocket, turning him into the scariest werewolf ever.

"Prepare yourselves! The monster that lies ahead
is sure to spook you out of your socks!" he warned.

"Behold Frankenstein!" Zac said. "I borrowed
my grandma's plastic Santa and painted it green."
Leah and the genies were impressed.

"I hope it's enough to win the Best Haunted House contest," Zac said. "But just to make sure, I'm going to check out the other houses."

As Zac left, he bumped into a stack of pumpkins. They rolled across the yard, knocking into other decorations and ruining his haunted house!

"Oh, no!" cried Leah. "He worked so hard to get ready for the contest. If only we could help him."

Shimmer smiled. "You can make a wish!"

"I wish for Zac's house to be decorated!" Leah said.
Shimmer used her genie magic to decorate the house, but
she didn't make it spooky. It looked like a big birthday cake!
"Oh, candy corns!" said Shimmer. "My mistake."

Leah used her second wish to fix Shimmer's mistake. Suddenly, the house was decorated with super-spooky bats and tombstones.

"Now, *this* is more like it!" said Leah.

Everything was perfect—except there was a real Frankenstein monster in Zac's yard!

The monster was friendly, but he liked to squish pumpkins and knock over decorations. He marched off, making a wreck of the neighborhood. "We have to get him back before anybody realizes he's a real monster!" said Leah. She and the genies followed the monster's messy trail.

As the friends chased the Frankenstein, they also straightened up his mess.

"I love cleaning!" Shimmer exclaimed as her handheld vacuum sucked up the pumpkin goo.

At the same time, Shine magically replaced
Zac's damaged pumpkins.

Soon the neighborhood was clean again, and the friends had found the monster.

"I wish we could just stop Frankenstein!" said Leah.

Shimmer immediately granted the wish—or at least, she tried to.

Suddenly, a giant sticky web appeared in front of the monster, but it wasn't strong enough to stop him. He walked through it as though it were cotton candy.

Just then, Frankenstein noticed that a spider
from Shimmer's web was on his shoulder.
"Frankenstein no like spiders!" he cried.

"It's okay, Frank," said Shine. "You don't need to be scared of this little guy. He's nice."

Then the monster wasn't afraid of the spider—in fact, they liked each other! That gave Leah an idea: she got Frankenstein to follow the spider safely back to Zac's house.

Zac ran up the street with a trophy in his hand. "I won the Best Haunted House contest! They said I had the best monster on the street!"

Then Zac saw Frankenstein. "Whoa! I don't remember my green Santa looking like *this*!" He shrugged. "But it's Halloween. Spooky things happen. A lot."

Leah thanked Shimmer and Shine for their help. "Even with the mistakes we made today, this was my favorite Halloween ever!"

"Mine too!" said Shimmer. "We got to meet Frankenstein and decorate. We are two lucky genies."

Shimmer and Shine hopped onto their magic carpet and soared off, counting down the days until the next Halloween.

HOWL FOR HALLOWEEN!

Adapted by David Lewman

Based on the teleplay "The Pups and
the Ghost Pirate" by Ursula Ziegler Sullivan

Illustrated by Nate Lovett

It was Halloween at the Lookout, and the PAW Patrol was excitedly preparing for the big night.

"Dressing up in costume is my favorite part of Halloween," said Princess Skye.

"My favorite part is trick-or-treating!" said Pirate Zuma. *"Arr!"*

But there was one thing they agreed on: they were both looking forward to Cap'n Turbot's ghost ship party!

They say the ship is haunted," said Skye. "It sounds super scary."
"Aww, that's only scary if you believe in ghosts," Zuma replied.
Suddenly, they heard a spooky wailing sound, and a ghost fluttered
down next to Zuma! The pirate pup yelped and jumped into the air.

"That's not a real ghost," Skye said with a giggle. "That's just Chase hanging a decoration."

"Told you there's no such thing as ghosts," Zuma said, though he was shaking.

Outside the Lookout, Rocky, Marshall, and Rubble had found a huge pumpkin to carve. Rocky cut the top with his Super Jack-o'-Lantern Scooper, and Marshall tried to pull it off. He tugged and tugged until it popped off the pumpkin . . .

. . . and landed on Rubble's head!

"This goo in my do makes me blue," said Rubble with a chuckle.

Meanwhile, Cap'n Turbot welcomed his first guests to the old pirate ship. Mayor Goodway and Chickaletta, Katie and Cali, and Mr. Porter and his grandson, Alex, all wore wonderful costumes. Mr. Porter had brought delicious Halloween cookies, and everyone told Cap'n Turbot they liked the spooky way he had decorated the boat.

"Thank you," he said. "Just trying to be the host with the most ghosts. Legend has it that this pirate vessel once sailed the waters of Adventure Bay with a ghost crew! *Mwah-ha-ha-ha!*"

Alex was a little scared. He tugged at his grandpa's sleeve. "Is the ship really haunted?" he asked.

"No," said Mr. Porter. "It's fun to play at being scared sometimes. There's no such thing as ghosts."

But if there were no ghosts on board, Mr. Porter wondered, who had eaten all his Halloween cookies?

And Katie wondered what was making that spooky moaning sound.

Later, while Cali was chasing a pesky seagull around the ship, she accidentally pulled on a rope that raised a sail.

Mayor Goodway was spooked. "Why is that sail going up on its own?" she asked.

Then the ship started to move! As the boat sailed away, the gangplank collapsed and Cap'n Turbot fell into the water! The pirate ship was headed out to sea—with no one at the helm!

"I seemed to have misplaced my glasses in the ocean," Cap'n Turbot said, rushing to climb back on board. But without his glasses, he couldn't steer the boat.

This was a job for the PAW Patrol! Mr. Porter called for help, and Ryder assembled the team. "Strange things are happening at Cap'n Turbot's Halloween party," he said. "Zuma, I need you and your hovercraft to catch up with the runaway ship." "Let's dive in!" barked the pirate pup.

"Skye, I need you and your helicopter to help slow down the ship," Ryder added. "And, Marshall, I need you to ride in Skye's harness to help lower the sails."

The team was ready for a *ruff-ruff* rescue!

Ryder and Zuma raced across the water as Skye zoomed through the air, carrying Marshall. When they reached the pirate ship, Skye slowed down and Marshall swung into the crow's nest!

Everyone cheered when Marshall lowered the sails.

At the same time, Ryder and Zuma raced alongside the ship. Ryder climbed out of his ATV and onto a ladder. But when Zuma jumped, he missed and splashed into the sea!

Luckily, he had propellers on his Pup Pack. He turned them on and shot out of the water—right into Ryder's arms!

The pirate ship was rocking and turning through the waves as if someone was sailing it!

"A ghost must be doing it," said Alex. "That is so cool!"

Alex might have thought being on a ghost ship was cool, but Ryder wasn't convinced. "There's got to be a simple explanation for all this," he said. "Let's check out the steering wheel."

Zuma and Marshall didn't budge.

"Oh," said Zuma, looking around for ghosts. "You meant us, too."

When Ryder, Zuma, and Marshall went to investigate, they made a surprising discovery: Chickaletta was perched on the wheel, turning it back and forth!

"There's your Halloween ghost," Ryder said, laughing. Zuma and Marshall sighed with relief.

But as Ryder was taking Chickaletta back to Mayor Goodway, a spooky moan came from behind some old barrels. Everyone was scared, but Ryder boldly walked toward the kegs.

Marshall and Zuma tried to stop him. "Ryder, don't!" they pleaded.

Ryder looked into the shadows and found . . .

. . . Wally the walrus napping behind the barrels!

"Wally's snores were echoing back here, which made the spooky sound," Ryder said.

When Mr. Porter looked, he saw cookie crumbs on the deck. "And it was Wally who ate all the cookies!"

Just then, Callie ran by, chasing the seagull. Once again, she accidentally raised the sail—but this time, the others saw it happen.

"Chickaletta was our secret captain. Wally the walrus made the ghostly sounds. And Callie raised the sails," Ryder said. He had solved all the mysteries!

He even helped Cap'n Turbot find his glasses . . . in his pocket!

Once they all got to dry land, they moved the party to the Lookout. There were games and treats for everyone. And best of all, the fun was ghost-free! Then Rocky looked up and saw something amazing.

A glowing pirate ship seemed to be floating across the full moon!

"I'm sure there's a simple explanation—I just don't know what it is!" said Ryder. "Happy Halloween, everyone!"